KILLER FISH

Russell Freedman

HOLIDAY HOUSE
New York

To BELLE *and* EDDIE HARRIS
who can tell some great fish stories of their own

Library of Congress Cataloging in Publication Data

Freedman, Russell.
  Killer fish.

  Includes index.
  Summary: Introduces some dangerous sea creatures
and describes the ways they kill.
  1. Dangerous fishes—Juvenile literature. [1. Dangerous marine animals. 2. Marine animals] I. Title.
QL618.7.F73   597'.065   81-85089
ISBN 0-8234-0449-8   AACR2

Contents

Great white shark, also known as The Man-eater.
ROBERT K. BRIGHAM/PHOTO RESEARCHERS

Why They Bite and Sting

Most fish are harmless. Only a few are a threat to people, and the chances of meeting one are very slim. Even so, there are creatures in the sea that can eat people or poison them, just as some tigers and snakes do on land.

Sharks are the most common man-eaters at sea, but they are not the only ones. Barracudas can be just as dangerous. The smallest fish known to eat human flesh are South American piranhas. They are a menace because they attack in packs.

Other fish attack people not because they are hungry but in self-defence. They attack only to protect themselves. A stingray will stay away from people whenever it can. But if it gets bumped or stepped on, it will lash out with its poisonous spine.

Along with different kinds of dangerous fish, the sea holds other threatening creatures like octopuses and jellyfish. This book describes the most menacing animals in the sea. Whether they bite, sting, shock, or grab, they can be deadly.

SHARKS

The greatest fear of any swimmer or diver is to be grabbed by the jaws of a man-eating shark. Luckily, this does not happen often. Most sharks leave people alone.

About 250 kinds of sharks roam through the world's seas. Of these, only 39 kinds have been known to attack people. Each year, between 50 and 100 shark attacks are reported from all parts of the world.

Sharks usually eat smaller fish. But some sharks will try to eat almost anything that moves. Sharks have devoured dogs, cats, horses, and cows, as well as people that have entered the water. In one case, they attacked an elephant that ran into the sea. They also eat their own kind. A shark that is wounded or dying will almost certainly be attacked by other sharks.

Blacktip reef shark, eating fish.
TOM MCHUGH/PHOTO RESEARCHERS

A hungry shark is drawn to movements in the water. It can feel an animal move from as far as 600 feet away. A wounded fish or a drowning person will quickly catch a shark's attention.

The shark zeroes in on its prey by smell. It has one of the keenest noses of any animal. It can sniff one ounce of fish blood in a million ounces of sea water. It can smell its prey from more than a quarter-mile away. And it can follow a scent trail like a trained hunting dog.

Nurse shark. NEW YORK ZOOLOGICAL SOCIETY

Sand tiger shark. MARINELAND OF FLORIDA

A shark's body is long and lean. It can cut swiftly through the water. As it gets close to its prey, it starts to swim around it in circles. No one can tell what a circling shark is going to do. Skin divers have come face-to-face with dangerous sharks and escaped unharmed.

If a circling shark is going to attack, it speeds up. It swims faster and faster in a smaller and smaller circle. Then it moves in fast for the first bite.

Because its mouth is far back under its head, a shark usually attacks from below. It jerks its snout upward, opens its jaws, and lunges forward for the kill. As it seizes its victim, it shakes its head violently from side to side and tears off a chunk of flesh. After the first bite, the shark may race along the victim's body, biting wildly. If its prey is not too large, the shark will gulp it down whole.

Bull shark, attacking a large fish.
MARINELAND OF FLORIDA

A shark has row after row of pointed teeth. Some sharks have four or five rows in each jaw. Others have as many as 20 rows, lined up one behind another. When the teeth in the front row are old and worn, they fall out. The teeth in the row behind move up to take their place. During a period of ten years, a tiger shark will grow, use, and shed as many as 24,000 teeth. Each one is as sharp as a razor.

Jaw of a sand tiger shark. MARINELAND OF FLORIDA

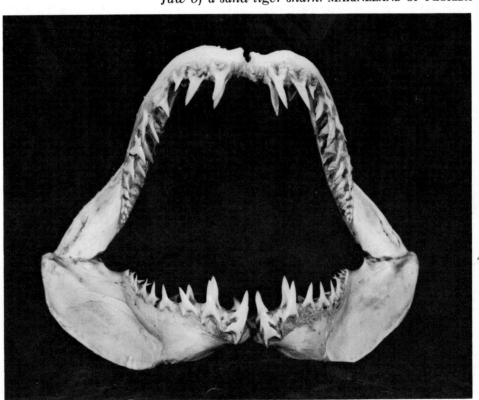

The great white shark has attacked more people than any other shark on record. It is known as The Man-Eater. Despite its name, this shark does not seem to like the taste of human flesh. After the first bite, many great whites actually spit out their human prey. Some victims die from loss of blood, but most of them live to tell the tale.

An ordinary great white shark is about 14 feet long. But some grow to be as long as 20 feet or more. They have jagged teeth the size of your thumb.

This great white shark was caught off Port Lincoln, Australia. It was 15 feet long and weighed 1,500 pounds.
SCOTT RANSOM/PHOTO RESEARCHERS

The tiger shark is the most dangerous shark in the tropics. It comes close to shore in its search for food. Tiger sharks will eat anything from snails to giant sea turtles. They also feed on garbage and dead bodies. In the stomach of one tiger shark, scientists found fish bones, bird bones, grass, feathers, bits of turtle shell, some old cans, a dog's backbone, and the skull of a cow.

Tiger shark. MARINELAND OF FLORIDA

BARRACUDAS

The great barracuda is known as "the tiger of the sea." It reaches a length of six feet or more—about the same length as a real tiger. Although barracudas are hunters, they seldom attack people. When they do, they can cripple their victims. In parts of Florida and the Caribbean, they are more feared than any shark.

A barracuda has a slender body, a pointed head, and powerful jaws. It has two kinds of teeth: long fangs for stabbing, and short teeth like daggers for cutting and tearing. A big barracuda can bite off a piece of flesh the size of your fist.

Barracudas are dreaded for their swift hit-and-run attacks. They strike without warning, take a bite, then vanish into the sea. The victim may never see the attacking fish. Many barracuda attacks are probably blamed on sharks.

Great barracuda. MARINELAND OF FLORIDA

PIRANHAS

A fish does not have to be big to be dangerous. Piranhas are small tropical fish that live in South American rivers. Some kinds do not bother people. But others, like the black piranha, are a real menace.

Piranha. WILLIAM M. STEPHENS

Teeth of a piranha.
ROY PINNEY/PHOTO RESEARCHERS

Piranhas have short sharp teeth like buzz saws. They usually feed on other fish, but they will sometimes bite land animals in the water. Like sharks, they are drawn to the smell of blood. They will swarm around a wounded and bleeding animal. Then they will actually eat it alive.

Large packs of piranhas have been known to devour horses and cattle that were crossing streams. There is a record of a 400-pound hog being stripped to the bone by piranhas in a few minutes.

Since piranhas live in distant jungles, lots of tall tales have grown up around them. Some of these tales are exaggerated, but others seem to be true. There are many reports of bathers and swimmers in South American rivers being bitten and even killed by these bloodthirsty little fish.

GIANT GROUPERS

Deep-sea divers have learned to stay away from the giant grouper. This huge fish lives along the sea bottom in the tropics. It lurks in coral reefs and sunken ships, darting out to gulp down smaller fish. Its enormous mouth acts as a suction pump, sucking in creatures that pass by. It could be called a swallower rather than a biter.

The biggest groupers are about 12 feet long and weigh about 1,000 pounds. They sometimes stalk pearl divers and shell divers, as a cat stalks a mouse. Occasionally they rush at divers, who must move fast to get away.

Pearl divers in the South Pacific claim that a giant grouper can swallow a man in one gulp. They tell many stories of narrow escapes. There is no proof that a grouper has ever eaten a diver. But divers have disappeared mysteriously in the ocean depths, and many people blame the giant grouper.

Giant grouper. RUSS KINNE/PHOTO RESEARCHERS

Southern stingray buried in sand. CARLETON RAY/PHOTO RESEARCHERS

The Stingers

STINGRAYS

More people are wounded by stingrays than by all other fish combined. These fish are found in shallow water along beaches and at the bottom of bays. They have tails like whips, armed with spines as sharp as daggers. They can not only stab a person, but can poison the wound as well.

Stingrays are relatives of sharks, but their habits are different. Their mouths are under their flat bodies. They use their teeth to grind up clams and crabs that live on the sea bottom. Like all poisonous fish, they use their spines only for protection.

Some stingrays are no bigger than your hand. Others are giants, nearly 12 feet long and seven feet wide. Even the biggest stingrays will never attack people unless they are bumped or stepped on. Since they bury part of their bodies in mud or sand, they are hard to see.

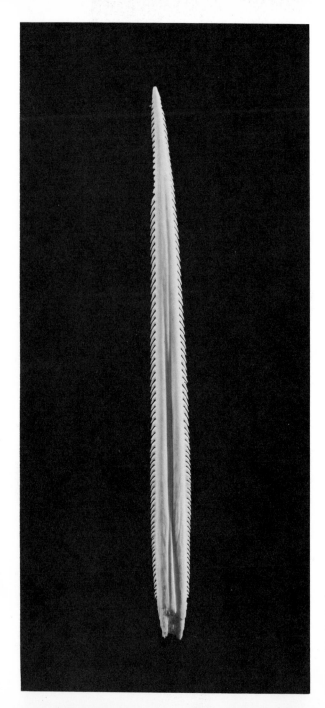

When a stingray is disturbed, it lashes out with its tail. It can flick its tail from side to side, or snap the tail over its head. It drives its spine into the enemy's flesh. The spine is notched with tiny barbs, like the edge of a steak knife. It is attached to a gland that pumps poison into the wound. Some stingrays have two or three poisonous spines near the base of their tails.

Stingray's spine, 6 inches long.
Some stingrays have spines as
long as 15 inches.
COURTESY OF THE AMERICAN
MUSEUM OF NATURAL HISTORY

Say's stingrays. RUSS KINNE/PHOTO RESEARCHERS

A stingray wound is painful, but it is not usually serious. However, some people have died after being stung in the stomach or chest by large stingrays. Anyone who is injured by one of these fish should seek first aid right away.

Weever fish at the bottom of a bay. The spine on its back lies
flat. When the fish is ready to fight, it lifts its spine.
TOM MCHUGH/PHOTO RESEARCHERS

WEEVER FISH

The drab little weever fish has been a threat to European fishermen since ancient times. It is only about the size of your foot, and it looks like an ordinary fish. Yet it has one of the most painful stings of any creature—a sting that can even cause death. In parts of Europe, it is called the dragonfish.

A weever fish has poisonous spines in the fins on its back and in the gills on either side of its head. When it is alarmed, it lifts its spines and is ready for action.

Fishermen are sometimes stung when they try to take these fish out of their nets. Weever fish are also a danger to swimmers, since they lie hidden in sand in shallow water. If anything disturbs them, they dart out of the sand and try to stab the enemy with their spines.

ZEBRA FISH

The zebra fish is one of the world's most beautiful fish. It swims slowly through the water, showing off its stripes and spots and lacy fins. These gorgeous fins are a warning. Hidden among them are 18 sharp, poisonous spines.

The zebra fish never uses its poisonous spines to catch prey. It feeds in the usual way, gulping down crabs, shrimp, and small fish. But it does use its spines to protect itself.

When a zebra fish feels threatened, it spins around. It points its spines toward the enemy and makes quick jabbing movements. Swimmers should never get close to one of these fish. At any moment, it may dart forward and stab with its spines.

Zebra fish are also called lion-fish or turkey fish. They belong to the large family of tropical scorpion fish, many of which are poisonous.

Zebra fish, also called the turkey fish because of the way it "struts" through the water.
MARINELAND OF FLORIDA

27

STONEFISH

Not all scorpion fish are beautiful, as you can see from this member of the family, the stonefish. Its body is covered with warts and coated with algae and slime. It hardly looks like a real fish. The stonefish is not only ugly, it is as deadly as a cobra. It has been called the world's most poisonous fish.

The stonefish spends its time hiding among stones and plants in shallow water. It waits to leap forward and snap up its prey. Its warty, slimy body makes it almost invisible. On its back are 13 jagged spines. Five more spines jut out from its side and rear. If an enemy approaches, the stonefish lies still and does not give itself away. It simply raises its poisonous spines and waits to be bumped or grabbed.

Stonefish are found along the coast of Australia. Anyone who steps on a stonefish by accident will get a painful dose of poison. Without quick medical aid, the victim may not survive. Some swimmers in Australia have died within an hour of stepping on a stonefish.

Stonefish. A. W. AMBLER/NAS, PHOTO RESEARCHERS

Fish are the only animals that use electricity as a weapon. About 250 kinds of fish are able to send an electrical charge into the water. The most powerful of these are electric rays and electric eels. They are the only ones that can harm people.

ELECTRIC RAYS

Electric rays are also called torpedo rays. Like the stingrays, they have fins that look like wings. There are special muscles at the base of their fins that make electricity, in much the same way as an electric battery. Electric rays are able to stun enemies and electrocute the small fish they feed on.

The biggest electric ray is the Atlantic torpedo, which can be six feet long. It lives in the Atlantic Ocean and the Mediterranean Sea. A large torpedo ray can send out up to 220 volts of electricity. That's twice the amount used in most homes, more than enough to knock a person down. It's enough to stun and possibly drown a swimmer who touches a torpedo ray or even comes close.

Atlantic torpedo ray.
NEW YORK ZOOLOGICAL SOCIETY

ELECTRIC EELS

The electric eel of South America is the most powerful of all electric fish. It lives in streams and swamps in the tropics. It can grow to be as long as nine feet. Its body is packed with 6,000 electric cells that can cause a shock of 650 volts—enough to stun a horse. A person standing in the water next to an electric eel would be knocked out by the charge.

The electric eel hides during the day and hunts at night. As it cruises along, it sends out a weak electric current. This helps it find its way and avoid enemies. It gives off a powerful current when it is alarmed or when it finds the fish and frogs it eats.

In experiments, electric eels have been wired up to make light bulbs flash. They have also been able to send sounds through loudspeakers. With a brief surge of power, an electric eel can light up more than 200 neon bulbs. It can make nearly twice the power needed to turn on an electric stove.

Preparing an electric eel for an experiment. The scientist wears rubber gloves for protection against shock. This eel is 6 feet, 5 inches long and weighs 45 pounds.
NEW YORK ZOOLOGICAL SOCIETY

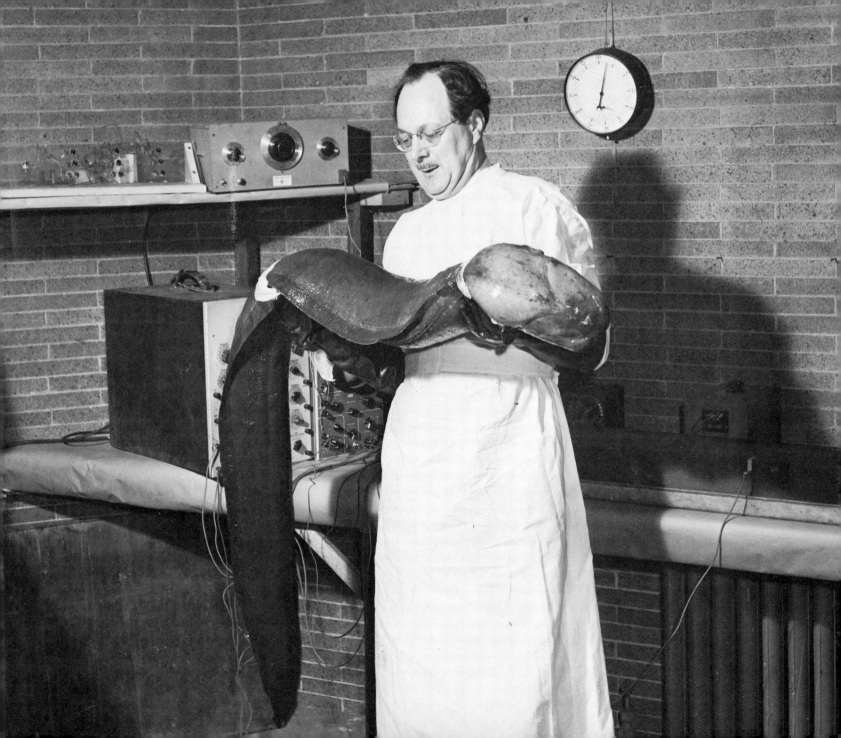

The Grabbers

OCTOPUSES

In adventure stories, the octopus is often a gruesome monster that wraps its rubbery arms around divers and carries them away. In real life, the octopus isn't nearly that dangerous. It is a shy, timid creature that usually flees from humans.

An octopus spends most of its time hiding among rocks. When it spots a fish, it reaches out with its eight arms, or tentacles. Each tentacle is lined with suction cups. The octopus grabs its prey, pulls it up to its mouth, and bites it to death.

Most octopuses are small, although some are giants with tentacles that are more than 25 feet long. A big octopus can hold a man underwater until he drowns. But that rarely if ever happens.

An octopus may bite to protect itself. Some of them have a poisonous bite. Oddly enough, the most deadly octopus is one of the smallest—the blue-ringed octopus. It is about the size of a saucer. This little creature has bitten many swimmers along the coast of Australia. It has caused at least two deaths. It's the only octopus that can truly be called a killer.

Blue-ringed octopus at the bottom of a rock pool.
A. B. JOYCE/PHOTO RESEARCHERS

Tentacles of a giant Pacific octopus. The octopus belongs to a group of animals called cephalopods (SEF-uh-luh-pods).
STEINHART AQUARIUM, SAN FRANCISCO

GIANT SQUIDS

The giant squid is one of the most mysterious animals in the ocean. Sailors have told tales about these creatures for centuries. Yet few giant squids have been seen alive, since they live in the darkest depths of cold northern seas.

Every so often, the dead body of a giant squid is washed up on a beach. The biggest one ever found was 55 feet long, including its tentacles. That's almost as long as a bowling alley.

A squid's body is shaped like a torpedo. Two long tentacles and eight shorter ones, lined with powerful suction cups, reach out from its head. Small squids are common in both the Atlantic and Pacific oceans. They will sometimes bite a fisherman's hand, but they are not really dangerous. Giant squids, however, are big enough to fight with killer whales. Whales have been found with terrible scars caused by the tentacles of giant squids.

Giant squids have been known to attack fishing boats with their tentacles. According to some reports, these creatures are man-eaters. During World War II, a giant squid appeared in the sea after a British troopship was torpedoed. It grabbed a survivor who was clinging to a life raft and pulled him down into the depths.

Remains of a giant squid found on a Massachusetts beach in 1980. Its brick-red outer skin was mostly gone. What was left of the squid weighed 430 pounds. Its original length was about 30 feet. Squids, like octopuses, are cephalopods. NEW ENGLAND AQUARIUM, BOSTON

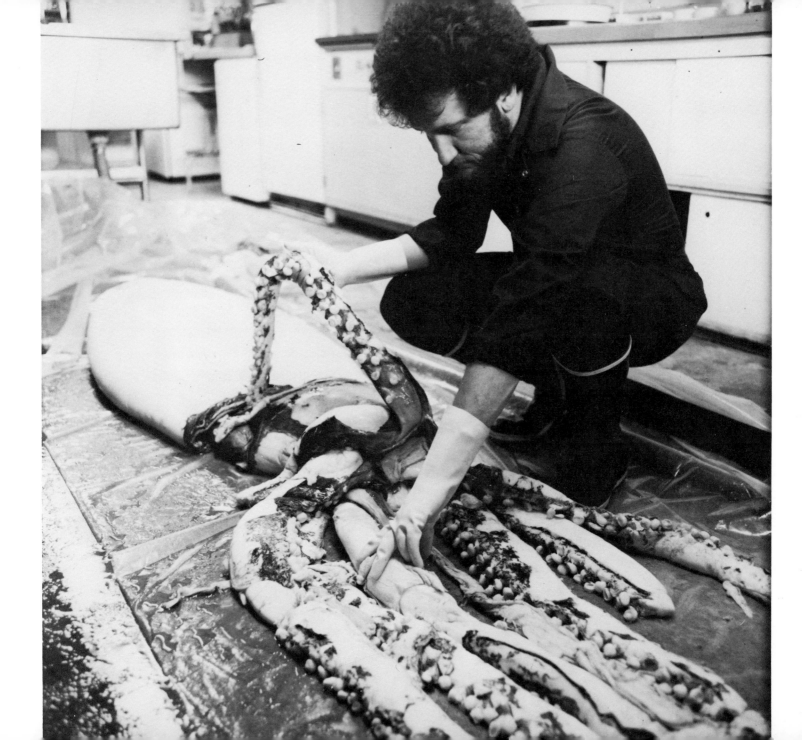

JELLYFISH

Some jellyfish are no bigger than a pea. Others are gigantic blobs. The giant jellyfish of the Arctic measures eight feet across the top of its see-through body. It has 800 tentacles. They hang down into the water as far as 200 feet—making it the longest animal on earth.

A jellyfish uses its tentacles to capture food. Each tentacle is armed with poisonous barbs. When a fish brushes against the tentacles, the sharp barbs shoot into its flesh. Then the sticky tentacles wrap around the fish and pull it up to the jellyfish's mouth.

Since a jellyfish may sting anything that touches it, swimmers should always keep their distance. Any jellyfish, no matter how small, can cause an uncomfortable skin rash. And some, like the common sea nettle, can deliver a painful sting.

The most dangerous jellyfish are the sea wasps found off the coast of Australia. They have jelly sacs the size of a human head and tentacles as long as 20 feet. A sea wasp is more poisonous than any snake. Its venom can paralyze a person's heart in a few minutes. People stung by sea wasps close to shore have collapsed and died before they could stagger back to the beach. That's why the sea wasp has been called the deadliest creature alive.

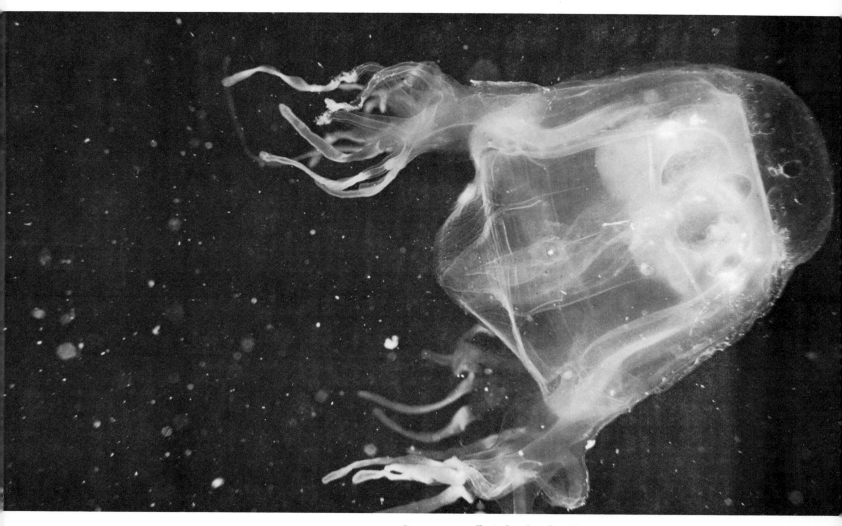

Sea wasp jellyfish, the deadliest creature in the sea. At least 70 people in Australia have been killed by sea wasps in this century. Jellyfish belong to a group of animals called coelenterates (seh-LEN-tuh-rates).